# MEET ALL THESE FRIENDS IN BUZZ BOOKS:

Thomas the Tank Engine
The Animals of Farthing Wood
Biker Mice From Mars
James Bond Junior
Fireman Sam
Joshua Jones
Rupert
Babar

First published in Great Britain 1994 by Buzz Books,
an imprint of Reed Children's Books
Michelin House, 81 Fulham Road, London SW3 6RB
and Auckland, Melbourne, Singapore and Toronto

ISBN 1 85591 390 9

Printed in Italy by Olivotto

# Badger in Danger

Story by Colin Dann
Text by Mary Risk
Illustrations by The County Studio

Winter held White Deer Park in its freezing grip. Snow lay deep on the ground, and the pond was covered with ice.

The Farthing Wood animals were cold and hungry. There was little food to be had, and Fox, Vixen and Badger had grown thin.

Toad and Adder had gone underground to hibernate, and in his set, Badger tried to fall asleep too. He wasn't a hibernating animal, but he was tired just the same.

"Badger! Are you all right?" squeaked Mole, who had come to check on him.

"All well, old friend?" said Fox, who had dropped in too.

"If only I could get some sleep," grumbled Badger. "I'm not so young any more."

He shut his eyes again, but still sleep
wouldn't come.

"I may as well go out and look for food,"
he told Mole.

Outside, the world was still. Icicles hung
from the trees. Nothing moved except
Badger, who set off slowly across the wood.
The snow clung to his fur, and he felt the
cold air all through his body.

"I'm getting old," he thought.

Suddenly, the ground seemed to give way beneath Badger's feet, and he fell down and down until he landed at the bottom of a ditch.

A terrible pain shot through his leg. He tried to stand, but couldn't.

"Help!" he called weakly. "Help!"

But he knew that no one would hear him.

Mole became worried when Badger didn't return. He went to tell Fox and the others.

"Badger's lost!" he said to his friends. "He went out to look for food, and...and..."

"But it's snowing!" said Mother Rabbit in a panic. "Badger might die!"

"I might die!" moaned Father Rabbit. "Doesn't anyone care about me?"

"Do be quiet," said Owl grumpily. "I must say, I'm worried about Badger, too."

"Then stop squabbling!" said Fox. "We must all go out and look for Badger."

There was a long silence.

"I'll go," said Kestrel.

"So will I!" said Mole. "Oh Badger! Badger!" and he began to cry.

For a long time, Badger lay still.

"This is it. The end," he thought.

Suddenly, a shadow fell across him. He glanced up to find a man looking down at him. Badger shivered, waiting for the blow to fall. Then he heard a soft, gentle voice.

"Hurt yourself have you, poor old boy? Hmm. Looks like a broken leg."

Badger felt himself being gently lifted up. He shut his eyes and played dead.

When he opened his eyes, he was in a
strange room. The man was pulling at his
painful leg, tying something round it.

Badger bared his teeth and growled, but
the man spoke softly, and stroked his head.

"He's trying to help me!" thought Badger.

14

He suddenly felt weak, and very, very tired. He shut his eyes again, and found that he could sleep after all.

When he woke, he felt warm and comfortable. A bowl of raw mince was on the floor beside him and he ate greedily.

"You smell of the wild," said a rude voice.

Badger looked up. A cat was watching him.

"I am wild," said Badger. "I grew up in Farthing Wood."

"Where's that?" asked Cat.

"It's a long story," said Badger, and he told Cat the story of his journey from Farthing Wood to White Deer Park.

Weeks passed. Slowly, Badger's leg healed.
He lay in his comfortable basket and talked
to Cat about his adventures with his friends
from Farthing Wood.

"And now they'll all be worrying about
me, probably risking their lives trying to
find me..." he said.

"More fool them," said Cat coolly.

"You could go and tell them I'm safe and well!" said Badger eagerly. "Please Cat, will you do it for me?"

"Me? Go out in the snow? On my own? You're mad," jeered Cat.

"Then you are just a soft, tame, human's animal after all," said Badger softly.

"How dare you?" spat Cat. "Okay. I'll go."

Cat wasn't used to going far from home. She hated the cold, and the smell of the wild. She walked and walked in White Deer Park, but found no one.

Finally, a little black snout appeared.

"Hey, you!" called Cat. "Come here!"

Mole saw Cat, and dived for cover.

"Stop!" called Cat. "Badger sent me!"

"Badger? He's alive?" squeaked Mole.

From the air, Kestrel saw Mole with a cat.

"Kee! Danger!" she cried, swooping down and stabbing at Cat's back with her talons.

"Stop!" shrieked Mole. "She's a friend! She's come with a message from Badger! He's alive!"

Kestrel let Cat go at once.

"I'm so sorry," she said.

"Please don't be angry, Cat," said Mole, beginning to cry. "I'm so grateful Badger's alive and well!"

19

"Fine friends you've got," sniffed Cat, when she reached home at last. "They're all thin and starving, except for Mole. As for that Kestrel, just wait till I catch her!"

"Starving? Thin?" said Badger anxiously. "But there's enough food for everyone here. Why don't they come and live with us?"

20

"You don't live here," scoffed Cat. "You'll be off soon, now you're better."

"I suppose I'll go now then," said Badger, lumbering to his feet. "I'll bring my friends back here, where it's warm and there's plenty of food."

"Ridiculous!" sneered Cat.

21

The fierce wind pierced Badger right through.

"It's so cold out here," he thought. "I much prefer my nice warm basket at the cottage."

Mole saw him first. He cried with joy.

"Oh Badger! At last! I've missed you so!"

"Hello, Moley," said Badger.

He went into Fox's earth and greeted the rest of his old friends.

Excitedly, Badger put forward his idea.
"There's food at the warden's cottage, and
it's warm, and..."

"Sorry, Badger old friend," said Fox. "We're
wild, and we're going to stay that way."

"Suit yourselves," said Badger with a shrug.
"I'm going to live at the warden's cottage."

Badger ran out of the earth and set off back
the way he'd come.

Kestrel followed Badger.

"Kee! Kee! Don't go!" she called.

"Oh, leave me alone!" snapped Badger.

When Badger arrived at the cottage, Cat was at the door with the warden.

"I've come home," said Badger.

The warden was kind, but firm. "Sorry," he said. "You're fit and well now. Go home."

Cat purred and rubbed herself against the warden's legs. He bent to stroke her.

"Could you be a human's pet like me?" asked Cat.

"No," said Badger with a sigh. "You're right, Cat. I've been a fool. I don't belong here."

Kestrel had been watching.

"You're one of us, Badger! Come home to us!" she called.

"You!" hissed Cat when she saw Kestrel.

Quick as a flash she pounced, and her teeth closed on Kestrel's wing.

Badger shook himself, as if he was waking from a long, long sleep. The animals of Farthing Wood had promised to protect each other, and his first loyalty was to his old friend

"Let Kestrel go!" Badger roared.

He launched himself at Cat. Badger was
soft from weeks of easy living, but as he
fought Cat his old strength flowed back.

Cat howled. Finally, she dropped Kestrel.
Then, miaowing pitifully, she limped back to
the cottage.

The animals had gathered in Fox's earth.

"Oh Badger," sobbed Mole. "I need you!"

"In my opinion, he's no great loss," said Owl haughtily. "We do very well without him."

Suddenly, there was a scrabbling sound at the earth's entrance and Kestrel appeared.

"Kestrel, you're wounded!" gasped Vixen.

"Yes, but Badger saved me," said Kestrel.

Badger came in behind her.

"I'm, er, sorry," he said quietly. "I haven't been quite myself lately, you know."

"Oh Badger, you're back!" sighed Mole. "I'm so happy."

"Yes indeed, Moley," said Badger, lifting his little friend gently into his arms. "I've come home."

# Little Miss Muffet
# sat on a tuffet,

eating her curds
and whey.

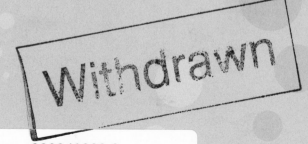

# Little Miss **Muffet**

## and

# Little Miss **Mumpet**

# Notes for adults

**TADPOLES NURSERY RHYMES** are structured to provide support for
newly independent readers. The books may also be used by adults for
sharing with young children.

The language of nursery rhymes is often already familiar to an emergent
reader, so the opportunity to see these rhymes in print gives a highly
supportive early reading experience. The alternative rhymes extend this
reading experience further, and encourage children to play with language
and try out their own rhymes.

**If you are reading this book with a child, here are a few suggestions:**

1. Make reading fun! Choose a time to read when you and the child are
   relaxed and have time to share the story.
2. Recite the nursery rhyme together before you start reading. What might the
   alternative rhyme be about? Why might the child like it?
3. Encourage the child to reread the rhyme, and to retell it in their
   own words, using the illustrations to remind them what has happened.
4. Point out together the rhyming words when the whole rhymes are repeated o
   pages 12 and 22 (developing phonological awareness will help with decodinç
   language) and encourage the child to make up their own alternative rhymes
5. Give praise! Remember that small mistakes need not always be corrected.

First published in 2008 by
Franklin Watts
338 Euston Road
London NW1 3BH

Franklin Watts Australia
Level 17/207 Kent Street
Sydney NSW 2000

Text (Little Miss Mumpet)
© Mick Gowar 2008
Illustration © Jan Smith 2008

The rights of Mick Gowar to be identified
as the author of Little Miss Mumpet and
Jan Smith as the illustrator of this Work
have been asserted in accordance with the
Copyright, Designs and Patents Act, 1988.

ISBN 978 0 7496 8036 7 (hbk)
ISBN 978 0 7496 8042 8 (pbk)

**Series Editor:** Jackie Hamley
**Series Advisor:** Dr Hilary Minns
**Series Designer:** Peter Scoulding

The author and publisher would like to
thank Frances Gowar for permission to
reproduce the photograph on p. 14.

Printed in China

Franklin Watts is a division of
Hachette Children's Books
an Hachette Livre UK company.
www.hachettelivre.co.uk

# Little Miss
# Muffet

**Retold by Mick Gowar**
**Illustrated by Jan Smith**

**FRANKLIN WATTS**
LONDON•SYDNEY

## Jan Smith

"Little Miss Muffet was one of my favourite nursery rhymes, because as soon as my mum said, '… who sat down beside her…' I knew I was about to get tickled!"

7

Along came a spider,
who sat down
beside her,

and frightened
Miss Muffet away!

# Little Miss Muffet

Little Miss Muffet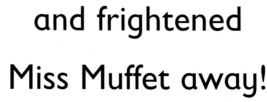

sat on a tuffet,

eating her curds and whey.

Along came a spider,

who sat down beside her,

and frightened

Miss Muffet away!

Can you point to the
rhyming words?

# Little Miss Mumpet

by Mick Gowar
Illustrated by Jan Smith

13

**Mick Gowar**

"This is me in my shed. This is where I write my books. When I'm not writing I like visiting schools to read my books and tell stories to the children."

# Little Miss Mumpet
found an old trumpet,

and sat herself

down on the hay.

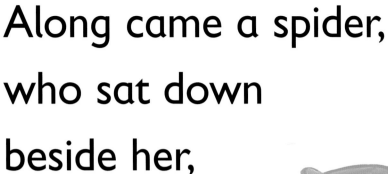

Along came a spider,
who sat down
beside her,

18

19

and taught
Miss Mumpet to play!

21

# Little Miss Mumpet

Little Miss Mumpet
found an old trumpet,
and sat herself down on the hay.
Along came a spider,
who sat down beside her,
and taught
Miss Mumpet to play!

Can you point to the
rhyming words?

# Puzzle Time!

Which of these instruments do you blow to play?

# Answers

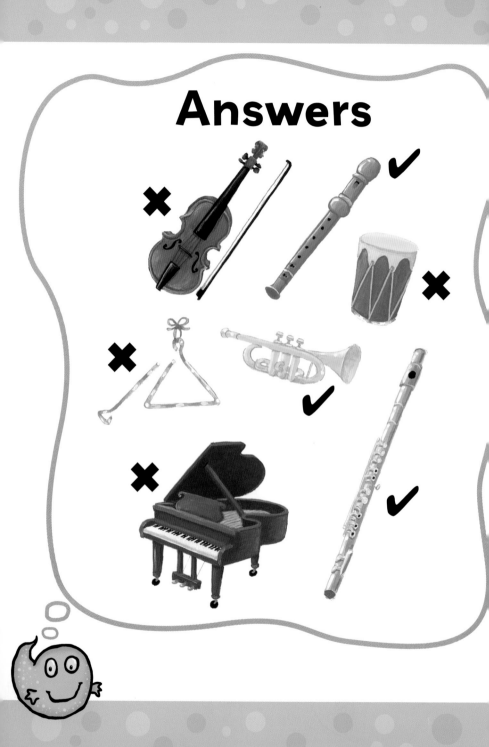